"Beneath My Flesh"

I0549550

Copyright © 2010 by: Gina-Nacole

All rights reserved. No part of this book shall be reproduced or transmitted in any form or by any means, electronic, mechanical, magnetic, photographic including photocopying, recording or by any information storage and retrieval system, without prior written permission of the publisher or author. No patent liability is assumed with respect to the use of the information contained herein. Although every precaution has been taken in preparation of this book, the publisher and author assume no responsibility for errors or omissions. Neither is any liability assumed for damages resulting from the use of the information contained herein.

Printed in the United States of America
Published November 2010

GINA-NACOLE

INTRO

I stared out of the window with irritation, wondering how I got here. As a little girl, I wanted to be a dancer and an actress. Funny how millions of people everyday tell children to follow their dreams. At the tender age of eighteen, you get taken off guard when every friend, family member, and dream thief will tell you, "time to grow up, go to college, and get a real job." Live the *"American" dream,"* just not your own. I wish someone would have let me know at five years old that it was impossible to follow a dream without becoming an outcast in society. At least I had managed to become a paid actress, however it was damn near impossible to make it a full time career. The work wasn't steady, but my bills were. I had gotten married at the ripe old age of 19, and it was a disaster. I had finally gotten my life together, at least most of it. At the ripe old age of 30, I was soul searching; trying to decide what I should do with the rest of my life. I didn't feel as though marriage was something I wanted to do again and I enjoyed the freedom that came with no children. I never felt that so-called maternal instinct to have a baby. Even though I was free, I felt trapped sitting in an office living in the nine to five world kissing my dreams goodbye. There was no stage, no lights-just a bunch of characters I wish would disappear out of this production called Corporate America. But it was a necessary evil. For a lot of people their passion was their children, their spouse, or their job. For me, it was my creativity. Anything that was artistic made passion run through my soul. My ex-husband was a mistake I made. I should have never married him. It was a tradition passed down to me from my parents, society, and all the Religious fanatics who bombarded my life with their traditionalist views. It was the thing "responsible" young women did. I felt punked into the institution of marriage and its concept. I felt getting married would rid me of all the horrible stereotypes I heard of unmarried women, even though my life as a single woman was not the wild life so many ignorant bastards classified all single people into. For me, it was freedom. I was not a feminist trying to make a statement to other women that marriage was horrible. All I wanted to do is live my life the way I wanted to without people harassing me about what I planned to do with my uterus. I enjoyed the ability to make decisions without "checking in" with someone else. I liked being able to wake up, and come and go as I please. I didn't have the obligation to have sex when I didn't feel like it, talk when I didn't feel like it, or have my happiness or unhappiness tied into another human being's actions. I hated the whole concept of being owned by a piece of paper called a marriage certificate. I didn't see enough happily married people in my lifetime for it to be such a forced issue in society, but I fell into the trap anyway. I was actually comfortable being by myself as a single woman, especially after learning what marriage entailed. A lot of women had public cries about the pain of their loneliness-posting blogs, writing in magazines, articles on social media websites, saying *"where are all the good men?"* I never judged them nor was I bitter, I just hated everyone assuming that I was looking for the same situation just because *they* were. Maybe because I was married before, I valued being single and I had yet to see what the big deal was in "tying the knot."

Sitting at my desk, it got harder and harder for me to be fake about my desires. I needed to fill the void that would free my creative energy. My life had become shiftless. I was a salary employee so overtime was not compensated, yet these corporate bitches wanted to add on after-hours work and evening meetings.

As I looked up, our eyes met. Ella, the bitchy department manager, was looking at me through the glass window sitting in her enormous office while I was sitting in a cube small enough for a raccoon. She was making sure I was working on her little "plantation" while stuffing her thin pink lips with a bag of Cool Ranch Doritos. I got up, walked towards her, and mentioned to her that I was going to lunch. After looking at her watch she nodded in approval. *"Fuck you,"* I thought to myself. The whole office environment made me feel like a slave, yet millions of people felt it was completely normal to have this system placed upon them to ask their management when to take lunch, how long they can be sick, and have their Human Resources department tell them three to five days was enough bereavement time to get over a loved one dying and report back to work. If indentured servitude was a part of life, I sure as hell didn't want to report to any Boss disguised as a husband when I got off work. All the Stepford wives would arrange their weekly Friday potlucks at work as if it was their right to enforce all employees to shop for food once a week for 25 people in an office I could care less about. As horrible as the economy was, I would rather give my extra potluck funds to starving people instead of the Betty Crocker divas in the office every week that already had a check coming in bi-weekly. When I got to my car, I contemplated running from the master's plantation and driving far away, never to return. But how would I be able to explain to my parents why I couldn't pay my rent? I had no right to be a burden on them.

I sat in the parking lot of the drive thru chicken shack up the street from my job. I was eating the drumstick in the most ghetto fabulous way just to insult my two-piece business suit that betrayed my true bohemian identity, and there she was. She pulled up right on the left driver's side of my red 2008 Mustang with her blond hair, ivory skin, and a self-entitled nonchalant smirk on her face. She had a stereotypical soccer-mom look with a red t-shirt and faded unflattering jeans. After she walked from the driver's side of her enormous silver SUV, she turned around and walked back to grab a notebook she had left on her passenger side. She carelessly yanked her passenger side door open, only for me to hear a loud *BANG* on the side of my car. She turned around at looked me directly in my face. I searched her eyes for an apology, an "oops", or an ounce of remorse-but instead, she rolled her eyes and turned her back to me as if I was invisible. Five years ago, I would have hopped out of my car and choked the bitch. The image of me pulling her by the hair and slapping her into next week paralyzed me to where I could not move. I let her walk away even though the anger had my adrenaline rising so quickly my hand started to shake. I felt I needed to have a ghetto moment before returning back to my formal conservative office environment just for old time's sake.

I wrapped my chicken bone in a napkin, drenched it with a packet of honey reserved for the biscuit I decided not to eat, walked quickly towards her SUV, and stuck it underneath her windshield. I did it all with a nonchalant smirk, the same way her enormous car door dented my mustang. It seemed better than beating her ass and taking out my frustration with life on her face. That's when I came to the conclusion that enough was enough. I called into work and lied about having a slight fender bender on my lunch hour. I couldn't help it. Hopefully the lie would buy me some time to think about what my next major life decision would be.

GIRL TALK

I had a date tonight that I was looking forward to. I crossed my fingers hoping he wasn't an idiot. I didn't really know how to explain my position to him on relationships so I hoped the subject wouldn't come up in conversation. If I were to hear a question about what I wanted out of him, I would be caught off guard. If I told him I didn't want to get married he would put me on a booty call list and make the situation too casual, or he would keep several women on the side. No one could accept that I was somewhere in between-I didn't want marriage and I didn't want anything casual. Both sides were too extreme for me. I tried to get my thoughts together as I went through my closet. There was no point in worrying if he was an asshole, because just about every adult woman will run across a no-good man at some point in her life anyway. If she already hasn't, she most likely will, it's not pessimistic, it's just statistically true so there was no need in avoiding the inevitable. So many women take the time to read books, magazines, and articles on why we get played or dogged out way too often. This is not to say *ALL* men fit into a negative category, because I don't think everything is true for *ALL* women. But society always puts most of the liability on the woman, as though we have the duty to train a man even if his mother didn't. In several states there are conversion laws where the wife can sue the mistress after an affair has been proven. Sue the mistress, and the man walks off after he does his evil deed? Where is the fairness or accountability in that system? Men decide when to declare war, the United States Government is primarily run by men, but somewhere along the way they are suppose to be completely clueless as to how to treat women. They run campaigns on television telling people of all ages *"just say no to drugs"* yet there is no accountability for men to *"just say no"* to a piece of ass. Society has given men in general a "pass" to be lifelong players. In their 20's it is brainwashed into a great number of women that perhaps they are just "immature", "sowing their oats", or they just haven't "grown up yet." But what happens when he is in his 40's? He's still excused from outside affairs and promiscuity due to his "midlife crisis". So I guess if you catch one of these bachelor's left hand after they are done screwing countless women, you are suppose to feel like you're the queen of the universe if they can pass HIV, HPV, and STD testing-then you can love the day you procreate with him. For some reason, I never thought this was a reward. Or maybe I had been propositioned one time too many by a married man. Funny how I never took the vow to save someone else's marriage yet I had to have the job of turning down an attractive man that chose to vow to someone else *he* would be faithful. The countless ads and media attention of the Single black woman made me cringe. I was so sick of having my identity dictated by society. Whether it was black people that wrote, "hmm you should be doing this or that cause you're a Black woman, or wear your hair natural cause Relaxers are the White Man's version of beauty." With countless uneducated stereotypes from other races including my own, it became a tiresome battle to wake up feeling on top of the world. I always wondered why countless *Girls Gone Wild* TV ads would show so many White women, how Hugh Hefner's mansion was full of blonde bombshells, and yet you would never hear *ALL* white women being stereotyped. I wasn't prejudice or racist, I was upset that I had to live with a double standard because of the color of my skin. I was upset that a White Woman's individuality and identity was able to be separated from the masses, yet as a Black woman I always had to be involved with someone's stereotype or perception of who and what I should be. I felt like I was a constant target as though I was still living in the 1960's. My hair had to be a certain texture, I had to be married by a certain age, I had to be maternal and want a baby, I had to still hear other Black people dividing the race by "light skin versus dark skin", and I had to have a constant goal to find "the right man". Guess it wouldn't bother me if that's what I was looking for or if they weren't making it a point to harass me just because I wanted different things out of life. Why can't people mind their own damned business? Let me not forget my favorite ignorant stereotype, "you sound like a white girl when you talk." As if speaking English was something I should be incapable of unless it was accompanied by constant neck rolls and aggression. For some reason, relationships themselves proved to be an overrated experience for me. There is always a desire spiritually for a heterosexual woman to seek the love from a man, and I was no different. My problem was being able to deal with the everyday upkeep of a relationship; I personally found it to be horribly uninteresting. I liked the beginning stages that took place when you met someone new-those feelings of butterflies in the pit of your stomach, the flirtation, and the enjoyment of being the recipient of a believable fairytale. But here I was against the norm, a woman of 30 being ostracized because I preferred being single with no children. I could've sworn this was a country that bragged on liberty and personal freedoms as long as you were a law-abiding tax paying citizen. Had this turned into a 3rd world country where simple things weren't a choice anymore? I wasn't killing anyone for God's sake. Even Gay marriage seemed more acceptable in society rather than a single Black straight woman deciding not to marry in this day and time. The judgmental elders in Church and the old-fashioned South automatically treated you as though you were some type of whore if you didn't buy into the typical two kids, white picket fence theory; even though adultery and unhappy marriages seemed to be an obvious awareness in the media and everyday life. These same bitches would cloud my brain with stories of themselves and their friends facing infidelity in their marriages. The way I saw it, I was already married once. I didn't like it the first time so I wasn't looking forward to doing it twice-but hey, you never know. I will keep an open mind just in case I meet a man that changes my mind. Unfortunately, I loved the power that came with the ability to walk away when I felt like it. I kept looking in my closet for an outfit that was sexy but not too suggestive for a first date. I was looking forward to Steven's companionship this evening. Steven had one daughter who was seven years old, was an engineer, and had an apartment in an upper middle-class neighborhood. He definitely came across as a gentleman the night I met him at a local Sports Bar downtown. I was watching the NBA playoffs with a few friends when I caught him staring at me. He walked up to me and introduced himself, then offered to buy me a drink. We exchanged numbers after he sat with me at the bar for an hour. After a few phone conversations, he asked me on a date. When I discussed the situation with a few of my female friends, we pondered on whether or not I should accept his invitation because he had invited me to his house. My friends Terry and Kelly debated last week one night at my apartment on whether or not it was a slick invitation for him to try and get laid, or if he was the fairytale prince he made himself out to be. He told me he wanted to cook me dinner and watch a movie. Was he being cheap or just trying to test me to see if I was a gold-digger or too "high maintenance?" I can't stand when men try to act like every woman is looking for a meal ticket when I go to work every day of the week my damned self. Yet the moment you tell them you don't need them they get offended. Damn if you do, damn if you don't. My friend Kelly was a hopeless romantic and always optimistic, so my skepticism was considered pessimistic in her eyes. "All men aren't the same, Erica. What if he wants to make you a romantic dinner so he can get to know you instead of going to a noisy restaurant? If he does spend a lot on dinner then you might want to worry about him expecting something *then*" said Kelly. My friend Terry was just as skeptical as I was. All I had to do was take one look at her scowl as she leaned back on my sofa with her arms crossed. I could tell by her body language that she considered him suspect. She cut her eyes at me and just said "Well, with all these men pretending not to be married it *would* be a good idea to scope out his place to make sure he's single, just make sure you carry a weapon in your purse." Terry had a thick Puerto Rican accent but I heard her loud and clear. I realized the truth in her statement. Having a bunch of dates out in secluded, quiet places could mean he had a secret life at home. Going into a crowded high-traffic, noisy area where our conversations would be screamed at the top of our lungs didn't seem too romantic either. I decided to go. Damn if I do, damn if I don't. If you give a man the benefit of the doubt then people can tend to be rude by saying that you didn't notice enough red flags, or either you attracted the wrong man because there is something wrong inside of you. There is always a judgmental ass random female around that acts as though they have always chosen a perfect man. Then there are the countless number of jerks that made sure they persecuted you if you didn't give a man the benefit of the doubt. "Black woman stop being bitter and stereotyping all men and give us a chance!" Or, "are you a lesbian or just stuck up?" I absolutely hated the plethora of ignorant comments suggesting you should be able to decode a pathological liar within two minutes like a professional physic. I didn't care what people thought, it just gave me anxiety to hear their mouths running all day with their bullshit in my ear all day. It made it hard not to have the desire to slap their mouth shut or run for the nearest earplugs to avoid the harassment. Even though I had a hefty list of associates, I only kept a few friends close to me. The people I hung around spent too much time trying to dictate my personal life and I was sick of them feeling as though I had to explain myself to them. I'm a grown ass woman, what I do is my business. I decided to wear jeans, fitting but not too tight to show off my size five frame. I wore my dark brown shoulder length hair in a ponytail and chose to wear small silver hoop earrings. I put on a purple shirt that showed enough cleavage to show him what I was working with, but not too much to appear sleazy. I checked my appearance one last time before I left my apartment. I made sure my doors were locked before I drove to his apartment.

I made it over to Steven's place in twenty minutes. As I knocked on the door, I became nervous. Was this just first date jitters or was my intuition telling me to turn around? I didn't have too much time to ponder because he opened the door so suddenly I couldn't gather my thoughts. He greeted me with a hug, kiss on the cheek, and a warm smile. Those dimples, *wow.* He had wonderful teeth, a sexy swagger, and an exotic appearance. He was a bi-racial Puerto Rican and black stallion with bronze skin, and a muscular 6' 2"athletic physique. He had a thin mustache, sexy hazel eyes, and short jet black curly hair that was soft as a baby. Without gazing at him too long, I looked around his apartment to follow his lead. "Have a seat," he said. As I walked over to the sofa and sat down I noticed I didn't smell one thing cooking in his apartment. "So what did you cook Steven?" He chose not to answer. Instead he smiled and walked towards the kitchen as I sat on the sofa. My eyes scanned around his apartment, which was spotless. I noticed the picture of his daughter and his Puerto Rican flag that proudly hung above his fireplace. Next to his daughter's picture, there was a photo in a frame of a Black woman hugging a Puerto Rican man that looked like it could have been Steven's parents. From the corner of my eye, I saw a plate coming towards my face. I tried hard as hell not to appear disappointed as I examined the bologna sandwich cut into small squares as if I was attending a cheap unorganized baby shower. I wanted to say *"take this shit back!"* Instead I mumbled "thank you." He sat right beside me and devoured the bologna sandwich as though it was a T-Bone steak. "Erica you're not hungry?" he asked.

"Ummm, no it's just that I'm ummm, allergic to bologna." I managed to tell that lie with a straight face. "Oh, I'm sorry! Can I make you something else?" he said. "Oh no, it's okay I'm not really hungry." I said. What a lie. My ass was as hungry as a German Sheppard but I would rather say I was allergic to bologna rather than tell him what was really on my mind. After all, if a woman tells a man she doesn't want a bologna sandwich on a first date, he still could play the card that the woman herself was too stuck up or high maintenance. I wondered how long men were going to assume that a woman had to lower her standards just because the ratio of females to males was in their favor. I didn't think I was "all that", I would just rather be by myself than be with bad company. As he chomped on the last corner of his sandwich he said, "*wow, you look amazing.*" "Thanks, you don't look too bad yourself." I replied. It would've been nice if he would have complimented me when his mouth wasn't open. I could see nothing but his mouth full of bologna and saliva-filled wet bread while he was speaking. Needless to say my eyes continued to scan the apartment, and I couldn't get my eyes off his television. I didn't see one damned DVD player. Was he planning on getting a pay-per view movie off of his cable service? I looked at him to make eye contact as he sipped on his soda. "Well I'm glad you came Ms. Sexy, so what do you wanna do?" he asked.

"Well I thought we were going to watch a movie," I replied. As he slid towards me closer, he said "Well, see I didn't get a chance to pick up a movie but we could watch T.V."

I didn't know whether to be pissed at the fact I had been invited over to watch a movie that he never went to purchase, or the fact that the aroma coming from him was completely disturbing. His breath smelled exactly like hot chitlins. I hated chitlins the smell, the look of them; and here I was with the aroma of them up close and personal. As he kept speaking, his words became ran together in my ears. I became discombobulated, dizzy, and I needed air. I was disappointed that this handsome man could turn into a hot breathing dragon within minutes. I couldn't focus on any words coming out of that shit trap he called a mouth. I was so busy trying to get my mind off of his teriyaki-fried ass farm raised chitlin breath that I was

caught off guard when he leaned in quickly towards me with his lips coming a little too close to mine. I was so startled I jumped, and the domino effect of my reaction resulted in my leg hitting the table, the plate crashing to the floor, and the bologna flying through the air and landing on his foot. I froze in silence. "Dang girl, I make you that nervous"? He laughed. "I'll get everything up sweetie, just relax while I get a towel out of the kitchen and clean this up real quick." As he walked his way into the kitchen, I bent down to pick up the stale bread that had collapsed on the floor. I had my head down while I collected some of the crumbs off the floor trying to figure out my escape. I heard footsteps coming toward me while he said, *"Hey sexy lady, I got a surprise for you baby."*
When I looked up, Steven was butt naked.

I must've ran so fast I could have broken every

Olympic record for the 200 yard dash. I was never so happy to hop into my red mustang. Freedom. Freedom from that hot breath. Freedom from that bologna sandwich. The worst part is thinking about how fine he was standing there with his naked body and looking up to see that his dick couldn't have been longer than two inches. I'm not one of those women that think I'm perfect, but I do feel I'm attractive enough to pull past a two inch dick. I wasn't looking for marriage I was looking for a situation. A situation where I could have companionship with one man, yet not combine my daily activities into a monotonous marriage routine. Why did I have to combine my finances, social security number, or bank account with anyone? I just wanted monogamous companionship and under standing with a special man. I didn't feel that was too much to ask for. Just an attractive guy whose breath didn't burn the inside of my nostrils. For some females size is not everything. A man giving me oral sex is great, but I held penetration to a higher value. After all, women have their youth shortened by the restrictions and expectations put on them even in their twenties. We are suppose to keep an ass of a Playboy centerfold. We have a full blown marketing campaign in the media by men that makes sure we have every moisturizer in the universe to avoid a wrinkle. We pay the expensive prices at the salon, we see the botox ads, the breast lifts, fake boobs... For men, as long as they have a good job and a nice car they are given a pass for looking as though a ton of bricks hit them. So I'm tired of women getting a bad wrap and being called picky just for having their own personal standards.

When I got home that night and pulled off my clothes, I turned on the water to get in the shower. While the water was warming up, I went to my sink to put the cold cream on my face. I started to get pissed off that I even wasted the expensive eyeliner and the expensive makeup powder I put on my face just to be cornered by a two inch dick. I stepped into the shower and my mind wandered. I had gotten Saved years ago at the Church I joined, but since I couldn't understand where I fit in; I stopped going. I wasn't in a position to lie to myself or God and pretend as though I wanted to marry, but yet I didn't want to go through these hellish dates just trying to find a reasonable convenient companion. It sounded selfish to some of my friends, but I had to be realistic. There was no title for what I wanted, let alone who or what I was. Each label on a romantic level was too extreme for who I was as a person. It seemed as though there should be an option somewhere in the middle. Even if I thought of a title such as a "boyfriend" It would require too much obligation. I couldn't handle the casual "booty call" either. With this day and age dating had turned into a sick game. A lot of people considered it normal to date online, but it frightened me. Once again I was an outcast in that arena, because I don't give a damn about technology or how it's the new "in" thing-I have always been a nonconformist by nature. I found it completely creepy to find any form of companionship by looking though personal profiles. That meant to me that dating was reduced to an online shopping catalog. "What age are you looking for?" "Do you prefer slim or athletic build?" Fuck that. It's not that I was old-fashioned, I simply believed the process of it all was unnatural. The internet allowed too many people to be too many things they really weren't. It was too fake, superficial, and with all the LOL's and LMAO's you couldn't tell who couldn't spell or who was just abbreviating. How is pressing "Enter" and clicking on a mouse prove if that person has any communication skills? The whole arena lacked so much substance. As I ran the soapy towel onto my body, I wondered if I should have just slept with him anyway. But as liberated as women feel, there are always double standards even if you are your own provider. As a woman, if I had sex with Steven or any man too quickly, it's my fault. His friends would pat him on the back and I would be the ho that gave it up too quickly. If a man has an affair, it's the fault of the mistress that tempted him or it's the wife that didn't do enough or give enough. It's funny that with all these double standards nobody likes to remember that if a woman and a man fornicate God is looking at them BOTH. So what if I did exactly what was taught by the Elders of the Church? What if I ignored Steven's breath and he never undressed? I would whisper in his ear that we would wait to have sex so that I could take the months and years to invest myself emotionally, mentally, and spiritually-just to prove to him I'm not the type of woman to be treated like a one-night stand. He proposes, we get married, and on my wedding night I discover that his two inch penis is something I don't want to live with the rest of my life. Guess I would be stuck in a marriage with sex I don't want. If I were to be sexually unsatisfied and cheat, I would be called a whore and persecuted. I wouldn't get the excuses men get when they cheat. I'd be an ungrateful selfish bitch that should be glad I was "taken" right? There has to be another way.

I stepped out of the shower and dried myself off. As I slipped into my pajamas I heard my cell phone ringing. It was a missed call from Steven. *Damn,* I hope he gets the hint and stops calling. The whole situation was so awkward I didn't want to even bother with a conversation. I decided to open my journal to write down my thoughts before going to bed.

"Beneath My Flesh"

As I flipped to find an empty page, I looked at my last entry and became disgusted at the déjà vu experience. It was dated a month and a half ago. It was a journal entry about Kalob. He was a 31 year old actor with smooth chocolate skin- a beautiful deep brown pecan color, 5' 11", and no children. I had met Kalob at an audition and our conversation was flirtatious. We decided to meet for lunch at a popular Mexican restaurant after the audition. As soon as he sat down to the table, he started pulling out all types of pictures and headshots out of his backpack and placing them on the table. I immediately thought he was way too superficial and stuck on himself. But damn, he had a right to be. He was a younger version of Blair Underwood, with deep brown intense hypnotic eyes. However, he wanted me to admire every single pose on his pictures while he rambled on about himself-his whole acting career, every modeling gig he ever booked, and how he wanted a large family. My brain thought of his admission of wanting a large family and I immediately stored him in the "temporary" file. No way this would be a long term situation, as I had no desire to experience childbirth. Having a cycle every 28 days was enough of a womanhood experience for me. As I looked at his pictures I saw the beautiful ripples down his chest showing his six pack. His abs and his arms were perfectly chiseled like a statue. Once again I had a fleeting moment where I just wanted to walk off and leave his pretty ass to talk about himself but I sat there anyway, not wanting to be rude. I had been so brainwashed by being called "stuck up" by men like this, that I thought maybe I was appearing to be inattentive. I had the common sense to know that a self-absorbed man's opinion of me being stuck up was irrelevant. Yet I felt the need to make sure they weren't seeing that side of me that could care less about getting too serious with them. I didn't want them treating me overly casual or with disrespect, so I played the part. As I sat across from Kalob, I could recall my male and female friends giving me advice that constantly contradicted every thought I had. My male friends would tell me to give a Kalob a clean slate. My female friends would bash me for allowing myself to be on a date with a self-absorbed jerk. At least this time I ended the date when he finished his meal, instead of having to escape by doing an Olympic 200 yard dash to my red mustang. He was so fine I decided to go out with him a few more times. I was hoping that maybe he was just nervous and wasn't *that* stuck on himself to where this was his normal everyday behavior. As I continued to read my journal, my mood became more depressed. There always seemed to be an ending to my stories that disgusted me.

"Journal Entry"

"I continued to go out with Kalob for a few weeks. He asked me if I could help him study his lines for a new production. I didn't want him to know where I lived yet so I stopped by his home. When I walked in, there was no furniture in the living room so I searched for a place to sit. He poured me a glass of wine and told me he would make sure I was comfortable. He went down his hallway and the next thing I know he was dragging an air mattress to the living room so I could sit in front of the television. As he stood there with his arms vigorously pumping the air mattress until it was inflated, I looked at him with admiration for his gesture of being a gentleman and making sure I was comfortable. He turned on the television as I sat sipping on my wine, ready for him to hand me a script for his show that he asked me to help him rehearse. While I was looking at the

television, he walked back into the kitchen. Like a cat, he came back and quietly slithered directly behind me after placing the bottle of wine behind us. Then he sat behind me, wrapped his arms around my waist, pulled my hair away from my shoulder, and planted a slobbery kiss on my neck. How in the hell did he manage to land a whole pound of slobber on my neck that slid down an entire hair strand? Gross! You've got to be kidding me. I yanked away from him and he moved from behind me. I thought maybe he got the hint by my obvious body language that I was totally not interested in fooling around with him. I tried to pretend like it never happened and asked him where the script was. He slouched down to his knees and looked me in my eyes in a flirtatious way. There was something about the look in his eyes I didn't like. I tried to get up from the air mattress but he quickly jumped on me the moment I made a move. His *knees were positioned between my thighs crushing my legs. He grabbed my arms and placed them over my head and I wrestled trying to free myself but he was too strong. The moment I started to scream he put his hand over my mouth. The moment I had one arm free, I grabbed the wine bottle he placed beside the air mattress in one swift motion and hit him over the head to get him off me. I hit him hard enough for him to fall backwards, but the bottle didn't break. I ran towards my purse and I could see him getting up. As soon as I opened the door he grabbed my leg, which caused me to stumble. Luckily I had the door cracked to where the next door neighbor heard me scream. His next door neighbor was a nosy middle-aged Italian woman that opened her door to see what all the screaming was about. As soon as he realized there would be a witness, he let go of my leg. I ran down the steps pissed off, angry, frightened, and humiliated. I couldn't even cry. I couldn't report a rape because there was nothing to report, and I couldn't report an assault. All the police would do is ask me why I was at his apartment, look at the wine glasses, the air mattress, and act like I "asked for it." Somehow when it all ended, it would be my fault...*

Reading the journal entry brought tears to my eyes. I was tired of being in situations where no matter what I did, I never won. Is the theory true that you are what you attract? If that's the case, how come I didn't attract anyone that was honest, caring, thoughtful, or spiritual? Or was it that because opposites attract I would be sentenced to a life full of ignorant bastards? I hadn't slept with Kalob or Steven. I was confident, never argued with them, never mistreated them, and I wasn't wearing, saying, or doing anything to suggest I was a ho so why was I being treated like a one? I wasn't desperate, didn't call too often, so what was the deal? Did *something* in me appear to be too strong to where they felt the need to tear *it* down? With the consistency of male dogs traveling my way from different careers, looks, financial backgrounds, educational levels-it seemed like I was still running into the same type of men no matter what I did. I closed the journal, turned off the lights, and got into bed.

New Day

As I drove into work that morning, I decided to turn off the radio and commute in silence. It was getting harder and harder to find out where I fit in. I felt the ghost of Harriett Tubman sitting in my car on the passenger side begging me not to go on the Plantation. I wanted to go to the Underground railroad where I would be free instead of going to my office. I could be free of the Corporate America politics and free from their ignorance. But how could I free myself from my spiritual confusions? Religion had become such a contradiction of my desires as a woman. Of course I didn't want to be in any situation where I would be going to and from different men, much less go through a lifelong torture of dating. But marriage seemed like a barbaric ancient institution to me. Cheating had become so normal in today's times and no one seemed to pull of monogamy. So why does everyone keep getting married? Were they following tradition like I was at 19? I guess I pardoned myself for my beliefs because I got sucked in the institution at a young age, but it was hard to imagine getting sucked into the barbaric belief system after age 25. My acting career was at a stand-still, the economy was so bad I was living in fear of taking risks to travel to auditions. I use to question myself less before the internet became so popular. Everyone on Earth that could sit in front of a computer had the right to dehumanize others for their color, complexion, marital choices, maternal choices, and career choices. It became increasingly difficult not to feel persecuted because now nothing seemed to be private or personal anymore with the internet. Someone that didn't like you could post a negative remark about you that a friend could see in a whole different state. People that you would never have had access to before social media networking could harass and belittle you. There was too much pressure. I was too young to give up, too old to dream, too independent to seek marriage, and too lonely to stay by myself. I was stuck in the middle and I didn't know where to go. My spiritual connection with God was strong but I had no desire to hang around people in my church that had a Bible verse to persecute my every indiscretion just because I wasn't perfect enough for *them*. I actually believed that what was good for the goose was good for the gander, so that went against their traditional belief system. I believed that both genders had roles in society but I didn't believe that decent human behavior fell solely on the shoulders of women. If women shouldn't sleep around I didn't see why men should be able to either. Was it just that deep in the Black community that there should be these constant posts on internet sites downing a black woman's worth?

I never saw groups of white men writing so many articles trashing white women or any other race for that matter. On many of the Black stations, every song seemed to talk of a man having different women on the side, yet they wondered why a woman would prefer to be single. I wondered if it would be easier if I dated a white man. The more I tried to stay off the computer to avoid these stereotypes the more I was forced to get on the evil internet that had managed to turn into a high-school bathroom wall that anyone could write on. If you want to look for another job or any type of opportunity you have to go online. Each time I sent out a resume and checked my email for a response, I would be exposed to the new stories on the homepage that made me feel even more alienated. There were countless blogs that would be seen on way too many sites. "Attention Black women: Do you know WHY BLACK MEN DATE WHITE WOMEN?"

"Because you're loud, you're arrogant, you're a gold-digger, you're too demanding." Wow, I'm glad I can be judged by so many people that never met me based on the fact I am black and I am a woman. Why can't black men date white women without cutting down black women? Maybe all the Black women should protest and just start dating White men. I actually had contemplated the idea because I did have an attraction towards White men. But for me, I always had the fear that in a heated argument a white man might slip and call me a Nigger. That would be the moment I would have to explain to my Mother why she needs to post bond at the county jail because I carved my initials in his forehead. As I pulled up and parked my car in the garage, I tried to feel blessed that I had a job in this economy. As I walked into the office and sat down in my cubicle, I turned on the computer. That evil trick ass computer with every demonic message

in life, available with just a click away. I wondered why the world loved computers so much. Yes, it was faster and more convenient. But you could also find out how to build a bomb, commit suicide, join a racial hate group, access pornography-things that you would have never been exposed to had it not been so easily available-it was disgusting. It would be time consuming for the average person to keep making trips to their local library to dig up such awful trash. But with a click of a button you could access sick bullshit all day. You didn't have to have any skills to be a producer you could simply pick up a camera and post your video online for the whole world to see without any talent. The phones in the office were ringing loudly in my ear and everyone was preparing for the stupid morning meeting that occurred daily. I opened my email and saw the message that my immediate supervisor had announced it would be her last day. Turns out all the responsibilities that we were splitting would be placed solely on me until a replacement was found for her. *DAMN*. No way in hell could I survive handling two jobs when it was hard enough to convince myself to be responsible enough to do my own. I scrolled through the other emails that included birthday announcements, anniversary announcements, and kitchen duties. *KITCHEN DUTIES*? The email stated: *"To cut down the budget for our company's janitorial staff, it is mandatory that each employee will be put on a rotating weekly schedule that includes taking out the trash, cleaning the dishes, and making coffee."* Why don't I just show up to work as Aunt Jemima? It was time for the morning meeting, and the women in the office were jumping around, high off their morning caffeine. The last thing I wanted to do was be in a meeting full of women, with the exception of one homosexual male. Before the meeting got started, I would have to sit at the table while the Stepford wives told their stories about their husbands, kids, and their nightly dinner recipes they would cook when they got home. Their world was so foreign to mine, we had nothing in common. Since they were aware I was previously married, they knew I understood the role of a wife; so they constantly bombarded me with their stories. They felt the need to pressure me to walk down the aisle again. They pressured me to have children. It's funny because I never pressured them NOT to be married so why were they taking the time to pressure me NOT to be single? I guess they felt as if my personal choice was their business or that somehow I was causing the world a serious change by my refusal to reproduce. I understood the role of a wife and still I never bashed marriage, I just didn't like it for *ME*. I was sick of them imposing their views on me while I sat there feeling attacked. *"Erica, when are you going to have babies? Erica, don't you want to get married again? Erica, men are going to think something is wrong with you if you're single. Erica, in the Bible it says women are suppose to be fruitful and multiply."* To say these women were married, I had no idea why they kept tabs on what I chose to do with my vagina. What if I flipped the script on them and read to them the parts of the Bible to debate them? *In the Bible, Corinthians states that its good for a man not to marry. In times of singleness, without the constraints of a family, a person can be available to be used by God anywhere and at any time. The gift of singleness is mentioned in 1 Corinthians 7 about the ability to be content without marriage.* I didn't even go there, I was tired of being harassed about why I didn't chose to marry. Marriage made me feel trapped, just like this damned job. Why did it always have to be "single" versus "married"?

Why couldn't it simply be that I made a choice for MY life just like they made a choice for THEIR life? Adults were nothing but the same bullies in junior high school that tried to force you into things you weren't interested in just so you can feel like you needed to "fit in". It made me upset that every since I could remember, I loved reading Black literature. It was one of my favorite hobbies that I no longer had as an outlet to relax. The last few years, all I saw was ignorance, judgment, and negativity on Black women. It made me feel embarrassed, harassed, rejected, ugly, angry, and bullied. They acted as if single black women with no children was life-threatening, even though they talked noise about the Black women that had too many children anyways. No matter what, there was always the negativity. "Erica, do you have any questions?" "Umm, no I don't", I said. I had completely blanked out with all the jabbering and hadn't even realized the meeting had started, and obviously it was coming to a close.

The department Manager, Ella, looked into my eyes as if she could see that I had not been paying attention. "Erica, if you don't mind I would like to see you in my office." The rest of the employees in the meeting scattered like roaches and swiftly ran back into their cubicles. I walked into Ella's office and sat in the chair across from her. She had a look of disappointment in her face. "Erica, as you know, you are the main point of contact. You didn't tell headquarters what the bill rate was or give them any information for their new employee. That is *your* job as a recruiter."

I was baffled. Rebecca, my immediate supervisor in my department, was the one who announced she was leaving-she was also the one who was supposed to have handled that particular requisition. Obviously, since she was leaving she had decided to transfer everything to me, including the requisitions she was suppose to handle before her resignation. I would be left with Ella, the potato chip crunching, arrogant ass Department Manager. She would micromanage my every move to make sure I was keeping up with my new 50% increase in job duties.

"Erica, do you not *get it*? You're just sitting there like you're deaf like you don't hear me! How come you're not saying anything?"

I wanted to say, *"Yes Bitch I got it, so stop talking to me with that condescending tone you overgrown, bacon-bit salad crouton eating fuckbubble!"* Instead I replied, "Yes, I will make sure I fix the situation."

"Well that's great Erica, I'm glad to know you can fix your mistakes. Now try paying attention to details. We're done here." She picked up her bag of chips and started munching on them in my face while staring at me, as she always did. Stuffing ten chips in her mouth at a time, wiping the crumbs off her 420 pound frame and washing down her chips with a Diet Soda. I despised Ella. I called her "Ella the elephant" under my breath all the time when she walked by my desk every morning. I sat there wondering why I didn't throw Rebecca under the bus. She was leaving anyway, but it would be her word against mine. In the end, if she wasn't going to be here, I would have to do it anyways; even though it was a requisition she was suppose to handle days ago. I couldn't help but stare at Ella. She had a thick moustache, and a face bigger than a Halloween pumpkin. She wore the same clothes three times a week, and she kept an odor. Ella had the smell of a purple onion with cheap perfume. Her light brown hair looked similar to a tiny afro because she had a cheap perm that was noticeably curled too tight, like a poodle that had been electrocuted. She searched my eyes for an answer as to why I was still sitting in the chair after I had clearly been dismissed, but I was frozen solid in the chair. I couldn't imagine looking at her for years to come until I reached my senior citizen years to collect Social Security. I knew I couldn't survive in this office much longer. The silence was at an unreasonable awkward level so I got up and walked back to my desk. I didn't want to face that I would be another washed-up has been artist in the entertainment business, but that's what I was and it was hard to face. I always wanted to be successful as an artist and see that proud look in my parent's eyes. The years of stress I caused them while being the gypsy that I was could finally come to an end. They would no longer have the worries of their daughter hopping from job to job. There wouldn't be the pity in their eyes when they looked at me hopelessly following my dreams like some lost little girl that wouldn't grow up. I returned to my desk and sat down, feeling like a failure.

The only success I felt in my heart was sitting at my desk with my head held high holding back my tears.

REMINISCE

After I left the office I just wanted to be by myself. I checked the messages on my answering machine. Kelly had invited me over. Terry called with the excitement that she would be getting a promotion at work. My friend William, a writer, had left me a message about a new project he wanted me to look over. I had known William for the past five years. He had written several plays, was in the process of completing a screenplay he wanted to film, and he wanted me prepare for a role he wrote in just for me. He was one of the best guy friends a girl could have and I didn't want to ruin our platonic relationship with any romantic thoughts of him. He was mid-forties, non-judgmental, and treated me like a little sister, and I needed him. William had always been supportive, always lifted me up when my spirits were down, and was such a gentle soul. On the next message I heard Steven's voice. *Steven the chitlin dragon.* If I closed my eyes and thought of him, I would remember his breath before his body. Everyone needs gum now and then, but his mouth was the worst smell I ever ran into. I automatically deleted the message without listening. My mind drifted again, searching my past to see what I could change to better my future. It's true, it's better to leave the past in the past-but I always thought of my past as a way to prevent making the same mistakes. William had always told me to live out my dreams. He would say, "hey, if I'm older than you and I haven't given up, then you have no excuse." William had recently been laid off and here he was still encouraging me, writing a script, and living out his dreams. He was the male consistency in my life, showing up at every birthday I had, just like he was my big brother. I wanted to take William's advice and follow my heart so I could feel peace again. I just didn't know where to go with my life in any department. Relationships, career, spirituality- I thought back to the day I had gotten Saved, how the Holy Spirit entered me and I felt renewed like I was a baby being born again. I needed to feel that peace again. I remembered the day as one of the most beautiful days in my life, even though getting Saved that day was a result of my divorce. I was 22 years old and I had been left with nothing. My marriage did not end because of the normal everyday circumstances, even though it would have anyways. I knew inside I didn't want to be married, but I thought I would tough it out. My parents were still married and so I felt the pressure to stay married, even through my unhappiness. Unfortunately, I didn't want to work it out, I just wanted to be free. I didn't want him asking me why it took me an extra twenty minutes to get home. I didn't want him rummaging through my purse just to be nosy. I didn't want him asking me for sex when I didn't want to be bothered. I was tired of him telling me what clothes I could and could not wear. I just didn't need a "leader", and I didn't feel like following anyone. I felt smart enough to make my own decisions. It seemed as though everyone I met was stuck in the 15th Century. I had *no* problem being submissive to make him happy, but being submissive never made *ME* happy. I was empty inside and tired of all of the "wifey chores". It was so normal for many people, but it bored me to death. When I asked my husband for a divorce, he went out drinking that night. When he returned, it was five a.m. in the morning. He woke me up from my sleep with tears in his eyes telling me he got drunk and ran into someone on the road. I immediately ran downstairs thinking he meant he wrecked the car in a minor traffic fender bender. As I examined the windshield that was cracked, I saw blood all over the hood of the car and on the seats-I immediately vomited. I could hear his slurred speech behind me, saying *"it was an accident! I was drunk I didn't see her. I didn't. I swear I didn't!"* He sobbed uncontrollably. Later, the police would come to take the car that was also in my name into police evidence, and my husband would be taken into custody. My bank account would be drained down to nothing after spending it on his attorney. I would have no apartment, no car, and I would see my husband toted away in handcuffs. He would be sentenced to twenty years in prison. I would send him the divorce decree months later. I wanted to be single and free again, but not this way. People use to ask me how I got over my husband so quickly. To the outside world I seemed insensitive and heartless. When he was incarcerated, I cried myself to sleep every night for weeks. I felt a heaviness in my heart, and I felt guilty for wanting to be free. I felt my prayers were answered in a devastating way. Just because I wanted to be free didn't mean I wanted him in prison, I just wanted a divorce. If I wouldn't have told him I wanted a divorce that night, maybe he wouldn't have been upset to the point of drinking so much. Then maybe he wouldn't have run into someone that was changing a tire on the side of the road and accidentally kill them. Unfortunately my landlord didn't care how serious my crisis was. The rent was due, she wanted a check immediately, end of story. My ex-husband's legal fees drained every last bit of my savings. I was broke, embarrassed, confused, and isolated. Even though many friends tried to be there for support, the fact that I felt no one could understand my pain made me feel alone and extremely depressed. I know all marriages aren't the same, but the entire concept that one person's actions can destroy someone else so quickly freaked me out. People said time and time I would grow out of it, but it became an institution I no longer saw a purpose or need for. Surely I could get the comfort of a man without going through the extremities of marriage again. Even though I was in my early twenties, I was clueless on how to date again. The rules and regulations were changing too much too fast. I felt as a grown woman I should be allowed to do as I please-but I was so sheltered at such a young age as a married woman, the whole dating scene was intimidating. Trying to have a crystal ball to see who liked me for who I was or who was lying in my face just to get a piece of ass was a sick game to me. I know other people get nervous or intimidated, but this was a deep fear that kept me in my house alone, until my eviction notice came. I was on the streets, and I had places I could go-but I was too embarrassed. I was too ashamed to tell my friends there was no money in my bank account. I couldn't tell my parents or siblings the severity of my situation because I was too proud. I had lost my job missing too much work during my ex-husband's trial. I couldn't even cry about the loss of the car because I don't know how sick I would have been driving it knowing my ex-husband was driving it the night he took someone's life. I went to a friend's house that evening to shower after I was evicted. I kept jumping from one friend's house to another. I was pretending I just needed a shoulder to lean on, but in reality I was trying to hide the fact that I had nowhere to go. I made sure I didn't stay anywhere too long and I made sure I kept a certain amount of luggage at each friend's house to cover up my homelessness. I kept my clothes clean, my hair decent-all to hide the fact I was dying inside. I never was the type that attended church on a weekly basis. But for some reason that week Kelly told me if I stayed in her guest room that Saturday, I would have to go to church with her on Sunday. After she drove us to Church I looked at all the well-dressed men and women going to and fro in the parking lot. I was nervous about going inside this perfect Holy building. I felt like I was such a horrible person. If I wouldn't have told my ex-husband I wanted a divorce, maybe he wouldn't have had too many drinks that resulted in a DWI manslaughter that took an innocent person's life. That burden of guilt was on my shoulder so deep I was waking up each day hoping I would die just so I could be taken away from my own misery. As Kelly and I sat towards the back of the Church, I listened to the choir singing and I felt a sense of tranquility. After the sermon was over, my spirit drifted to the Alter. The Pastor picked me out of all the people lined up on their knees in prayer, and placed his hand over my head. The next thing I knew I had spoken in a tongue that I had never heard escape my lips. Heaviness lifted off my heart, and I felt as though I was high. So this was the feeling that explained why so many people turned into Church fanatics and beat the Bible in your face? Even though people like that got on my nerves, I at least finally understood it. The feeling of peace I felt was so addictive I wanted to feel that sensation over and over again. In that moment, I felt whole again-Jesus touched me. I was not into organized religion because I ran into too many people yelling Bible verses out to prove they were so *righteous* just to condemn others. Their judgmental spirits sat in the front row each and every Sunday with their hypocrisy, knowing full well they had hidden sins yet still chose to look down on others. But I had felt the touch of Jesus and I knew I wanted a personal relationship with *HIM*.

Kelly allowed me to use her car for the next two days to look for another job. Luckily I got a temp assignment that was starting the following week. I felt that order was restored back into my life. With a job I can get another car, another apartment, and finally have money in my bank account again. If it weren't for me rotating from house to house amongst my friends I wouldn't have been able to eat. After sharing my testimony with my Pastor he gave me a donation of $200. Within three months I put a down payment on a car, put a deposit on a new apartment, and put $250 back into the Church's collection plate. I was also chosen for a lead role in a new show that was being hosted by a top local theater company. The man that I was in a scene with was named Cody. Cody was a musician that was a Pastor's son. He had the most innocent eyes you would ever see and an angelic presence. He had a beautiful voice, humble spirit, and he sung like a soulful hummingbird with a voice that penetrated you deep in your soul. He always had daily passages he would read from the Bible to the cast members. I cared nothing about what he owned or how much money he made, something in him was just beautiful. He was 6"2", chocolate complexion, talented, with a smile that was contagious and boyish dimples. He told me he was on the road at times with his singing career, and we repeatedly met outside of rehearsal to study our lines. Three months later, it happened. We were studying our lines eating strawberries in my brand new apartment and he threw one strawberry at me in the middle of my sentence. It was so funny and random I could do nothing but laugh. I picked up the pillow on my couch and threw it on top of his head. He looked into my eyes and the connection was undeniable whether he or I chose to accept it or not. He grabbed my shoulders and slid his tongue in my mouth, as he moved his hands towards my breasts. I wanted to stop him, but I felt as though I couldn't move. He slipped his fingers inside me and massaged me gently. He tore at the buttons on my shirt as if they were his enemy, and placed my nipple in his mouth. He kissed and licked on my stomach, and just as he started to put his lips in between my legs, I stopped him. I knew if I slept with him I would connect with him too deeply, and for some reason I was too afraid. He had done nothing but caress and kiss me, yet I already felt too close to him. He grabbed my hand and put it on his face, then wrapped his arms around me and held me close. After a few minutes, we went back to reading the script and rehearsing the lines-but the sexual tension was undeniable. After looking at the clock and noticing how late it was, I offered him a blanket so he could sleep on the sofa. I walked up the stairs and pulled off my clothes before getting into bed. I was wet, sexually frustrated, and mentally drained from fighting the losing battle to keep my panties up. I crawled beneath the sheets and closed my eyes. I now had the stereotypical pressure and oppression placed upon me to deny my desire, wondering if a test would be failed on the male dating checklist. Had I not waited long enough to sleep with him? Would he think I was a whore if I didn't pressure him for a commitment before having sex? I hated worrying about all of the dumb romantic politics. I was the type of woman that handled each situation accordingly and I didn't want to play anyone's rules besides my own. Unfortunately, when it involves someone you care about, you have to examine how you might appear in *their* eyes. I heard my steps creaking as footsteps entered my bedroom. When I looked up I saw his silhouette, and he politely asked me if I had another pillow while he moved closer to me. As I reached towards the empty space in my king sized bed, I handed him the extra pillow. Instead of grabbing the pillow, he grabbed my arm and pulled me toward him as he sat on the bed. His eyes were piercing through me even though my room was dark, with the exception of the street light reflecting off of the blinds through my window. I could sense he was on a mission to finish what he started and I had no more fight left in me to stop him. He pulled back the covers and planted kisses on my navel. He ripped my panties off and yanked them down to my knees as he put his face in between my legs and licked my clitoris repeatedly. As I grabbed his head in between my thighs, part of me wanted for him to get off me; but I was hypnotized by his tongue. No matter how hard I tried to stifle my moans, I couldn't. He sucked on my clitoris and slipped his tongue deeper inside me. I crawled backwards but his head responded to my every movement. His hands were rumbling in his pockets while his tongue was in full motion. He took the condom out of his wallet and quickly placed it on his dick. I couldn't move my lips to say no, because my body was saying yes, and my mind was racing wondering how big of a mistake I might make with him that I would later regret. The seduction was overpowering me as he put his dick inside me. He rocked me gently at first then his thrusts got harder, as he vocalized in a demanding tone to keep my legs open and take his dick. *"Take this dick. That's right, give me that pussy."* He picked me up and carried me across the room and set my ass on top of my office desk right next to the empty space next to the computer while my back was against the wall. My legs were wrapped around his waist, and he was thrusting me so hard I thought the neighbors would think I was in a domestic dispute. As soon as I felt myself near an orgasm, something went terribly wrong. I had forgotten that a picture frame was right next to the computer. I didn't notice that somehow in the heat of passion we broke the picture frame and there was broken glass stabbing my butt cheeks. I screamed in pain as I tried to free myself from his tight grasp. My screams were exciting him, and he thought it was because I was reaching an orgasm. I yelled for him to stop but he thought it was all part of the passionate act. The more I yelled the harder he fucked me. I was afraid my ass was going to look like a carved turkey after he finally finished. His thrusts became so deep I felt overwhelmed by the pain, but it hurt so good. He said my name twice and started to suck on my neck before he came. He kissed me on my forehead and went into the bathroom to pull off the condom. After I heard the toilet flush, I heard the water running and the sounds of him wringing out a towel to wash himself. My legs were still shaking and my body was numb. I didn't want to access the damages of my ass while he was there, but I had to. I was hoping he would turn off the bathroom light before walking into the bedroom so I could hide the damage done to my ass. What would I say when I walked by him if he was able to see that my ass looked like it had been attacked by Freddy Krueger? He came out of the bathroom, shut off the lights, then walked up to me and gave me a kiss on the lips. I ended the kiss quickly and excused myself to the restroom. *Good he shut off the lights, I hope he didn't notice any ass damage.* As I shut the bathroom door and turned around to evaluate my injury, there was a 2 inch piece of glass sticking out of my right butt cheek. *Soldier down! Soldier down!* I felt like I was in a classic Rambo movie. I turned on the water in the shower so I could muffle any strange noises or possible moans of pain while I performed my quiet surgery. I covered my mouth with my left hand to try to muffle a possible scream and fell to my knees. After I silently counted to three, I told myself I would quickly snatch the piece of glass out of my right butt cheek. As soon as I snatched it, I hollered and rolled on the floor as if I had been shot. When I saw the blood escaping my butt cheek I felt faint and dizzy.

"*Agggggggghhhhhhh DAMNNN!*"

"Erica! Are you okay in there?"

"Uhhh, Yeah, Cody, umm the water is just hot that's all." I hopped in the shower with my back towards the water and closed my eyes, hoping the bleeding on my ass would stop by the time I got out of the shower. For extra security, I held a washcloth directly on the flesh wound. I finished my shower, dried off, put the towel in the laundry basket, and I crawled into bed. He held me like a newborn as I laid my head down on his chest, and I had the best sleep I had in a long time.

Cody and I became closer each day, until the things I loved about him became the very reason I hated about him. He was an artist like me, so he understood my need for freedom and I understood his. But his unsteady income had become an issue. I had just started getting back on my feet so I couldn't, wouldn't, and refused to become a provider for him. I knew he wasn't working, with the exception of his singing gigs but I never wanted to judge him for staying home with his parents even though he was in his late twenties. He had a son and he barely worked, but I tried to stay loyal and I tried not to ask him for anything. When I recall what I went through with him, I get sick to my stomach at the stereotype that black women are gold-diggers. I tried to make sure I didn't insult his manhood by asking to go places he couldn't afford. And even if I could afford it for myself, with my new beginning I couldn't always afford to pick up the tab for him so I didn't want to start the habit of inviting him places and paying for both of us. I didn't want to turn this companionship into a burden on myself to where I had to suffer the consequences of his financial situation. The visits for the next few months were frequent, mostly sexual. But there were also times he spent the night and there was no sex at all. The show we worked on had reached its final performance, so we had no scripts to study anymore but we had great conversations. I was happy for him when his singing gigs started to come in-but his traveling also started to increase. He would be gone for months at a time, and the calls started to diminish. He would constantly tell me that he loved me, but it wasn't enough because my resentment for being loyal to him was increasing. I was the woman that never had flowers on Valentine's day, and only received a call or a text on a birthday. There was never even a card from him at Christmas. One day he had called me on his son's birthday (which was a few weeks before mine) in tears saying that he had no money for his son's birthday gift. I sympathized with him, but the little things he could have done to appreciate me weren't being done. I tried to keep him around to avoid accumulating another dick notch on my belt if I replaced him. Yet in his mind, his ego led him to believe that he was too hard for me to get over just because I tolerated him. But as time went on he started to become way too useless. In my heart my memory was stuck in the moments we shared when I first met him, but my mind was getting ready to exit. One night, a couple of weeks before my birthday, he came over and drove up in a brand new car. He also walked in my apartment showing me a $1500 brand new laptop that he boasted about purchasing the day before. This was only a week after saying he had no money for his son's birthday and ranted on and on about how cruel his "baby's mama" was for trying to put him on child support. When I saw these high priced items in his possession I felt disgusted and I tried to sneak in my comments indirectly. I asked him if the laptop was for his son and he answered *no* very quickly. He informed me that he still hadn't had a chance to pick up a gift for his son and calmly stated that he wasn't worried about it because the mother of his child along with his own mother had bought his son presents with their own money. I felt every Bible verse he would whisper at our old rehearsals chiming in my ears. The tall, handsome, spiritual, God-fearing beautiful man I adored all of a sudden looked like a tiny selfish bitch. Every word that came out of his mouth became the alpha and omega that could strike a match and light an angry fire inside of me. So should I have just turned my back on him once I knew he wasn't financially stable? Yes, I should have. It's a shame that women are called gold-diggers when they choose not to put up with this shit. I felt like an unappreciated idiot. All the love I had given him went down the drain and he was as phony as a $4 bill to me. I know all of us fall short of God's glory, but for some reason I thought he was more advanced spiritually than I was because he was a Pastor's son. I thought his morals were stronger than mine. I was tired of being accountable for a man's actions when I had to be an adult and be accountable for mine. I was too tired to calculate why or what I did to be this unappreciated. All I did was accept him and his situation the way I felt he accepted me for who I was. Perhaps I was no longer a challenge to him because I was loyal and stuck by him, gave him moral support, and picked his broke ass up sometimes before he had his fancy car-he probably felt he had the need to conquer someone else. It was a horrible feeling but I knew it was over because once I lose ALL respect for a man, I start talking to them like shit. I stopped speaking to him and I refused to return his call for a few months until his birthday came around. He called me a few days before his birthday and finally I answered the phone. We had a long conversation talking about old times, and a part of me missed the charming spiritual man I met once before. Even though he had managed to never buy me anything for my birthday I decided to try not to be bitter and end things on good terms. We had planned for him to come over on the night of his birthday so that I could cook him dinner, and I decided to get him a small inexpensive cake. I had a hard time bringing myself to spend money on him at all (even if it was a small cake) because he never spent a dime on me, but oh well. I called him and he text me back, saying that he was only fifteen minutes away. I set out the wine, lit a candle on his cake, and turned on the television. I poured myself a glass of wine and decided to lay on my sofa while waiting for him, but I accidentally dozed off. I woke up an hour and a half later, startled. *Had he knocked on the door while I was asleep?* I immediately jumped up to check on the candle I left on the cake, then I frantically raced around the house trying to locate my cell phone. I looked at my missed calls-not one from Cody. I dialed his number and it went straight to voicemail. I left a message. Ten minutes later I sent a text. No reply. If he's not dead, he's going to wish he was when I get done with him. *That twisted trifling, self-entitled Bastard.* I looked at the cake I had went to the store to get and I refused to let it go to waste. I got the knife and took a large slice, and devoured it like an angry animal. I was still pissed off so I devoured the entire chocolate cake. I walked up the steps to my bedroom and crawled into bed and fell asleep quickly. Hours later, I heard the phone ringing. I reached to pick up the phone and it was Cody.

"Erica, I'm so sorry I got tied up. I'm on my way baby."

"Cody, *fuck you.*" I hung up the phone in his face and went back to sleep. There was nothing he could say that would do any good, because I had mentally checked out.

Almost every woman I knew was living a lie, unfortunately I wasn't able to escape the statistic either. The ones who bragged on their significant others one year, had horror stories of betrayal and drama the next year. White women, black women, Hispanic women, Asian women. The older women that had been married for decades would filter stories out to co-workers of how much work it took to keep the marriage together after years of betrayal. No matter what woman I met for some reason we all had the same stories, so I wonder why magazines kept posting the articles on how to keep a man. Biology had played a trick on all of us because men are natural hunters. It was hard for me to believe they would give up the hunt after falling in love with a woman, because men had the primitive instinct to *chase*. This society has obligated women for centuries to wait on the husband of our dreams and save our virginity for the right man. What happens to the thought process when all the "Good girls" are getting played like everyday common whores? Is it fair for a woman to suppress all of her sexual desires and cross her fingers that the right man will come along even though he is out there having all the sex he wants? Why did society allow them such freedom that women couldn't have? Fornication in the Bible is wrong for both genders but for some reason there is no restriction on men pulling out their unholy dicks. Were women more emotional about sex because they were suppressing their desires so long that they became overwhelmed the moment they got some dick? I knew that asking these questions to a Pastor or any church member would cause them to find the nearest bucket of holy water to throw in my face, cast judgment upon me, misinterpret my philosophical analytical nature, or accuse me of blasphemy. What was taking place in this world and what was written in the Bible left me torn so I preferred to get out of the fairytale mentality. My name wasn't Cinderella so it was hard for me to believe in Prince Charming. But Cody had sold me the fantasy for awhile, and I needed him at that moment. Logically, if I didn't want to marry again then there might be a moment where he wanted to marry, and I wouldn't want to share my non-traditional anti-marriage beliefs with him. Besides, even though I found comfort in him, I knew we weren't meant to be. Perhaps something or someone would change my mind, but the more unhappily married women and flirting husbands I met, my skepticism remained. The single women that wanted to be married were doing flips to keep their men satisfied, and the married women were doing flips to keep their straying men on a leash. It appeared in my eyes to be a fucking circus. If marriage was the key to not feeling lonely then why is there a piece of paper that grants you a divorce? Why did I know so many lonely married women that had husbands who paid them no attention anyway? And if cheating was so "normal" in this day and time then it became evident to me that it was *LOVE* that kept two people together, evidently it wasn't the marriage certificate. What I wanted was to be understood, loved, appreciated, and accepted without giving up my closet space, freedom, co-mingling my finances, or being pressured to have children-knowing I had no maternal desires.

BACK TO REALITY

I went to work the next day wondering how I would be able to sit still and watch that dumb chip eating whale named Ella stare out of her office window and glare at me. I know how many times I had received the judgmental stares from friends and family and I didn't want to face a horrible situation like losing my apartment. To say I was an actress, it was getting harder and harder to pretend I could survive in this office cubicle that made me feel like a caged animal. I was searching for a place I could be happy in. I didn't fit in the box for a serious relationship, I didn't want to be a "booty-call", I didn't like my career, nor did I fit in with my family. I was just too eccentric for them to understand me. My family was very traditional, and I wasn't living in their familiar territory because I didn't want the white picket fence and the 2.5 children. I wanted to be like

Oprah-make millions of dollars, have a mansion, and have a Stedmon when I felt like it. I wanted to give to charity like Oprah. I wanted to be a producer, talk-show host, and an actress like Oprah. Oprah had everything I wanted including the dogs she owned. It wasn't just about Oprah's money, it was the freedom and the lifestyle of having a man when she wanted, but not one that needed to control who she was as a person. She had no pressure to submit, give up her dreams, or start reproducing because she was *free*. What could I say to all those Religious folks that would tell me I was wrong for how I felt? As I opened the emails at my desk I felt like a prostitute. I was selling my soul, burying my talents while I worked long hours, and being fucked for a check signed by the "Office Pimp," Ella. I felt like I was sitting at this desk behind a computer against my will, but I was stuck to the chair being pimped just to pay my electric bill. Why can't I slap all the idiots that claim women that like men with money are gold-diggers? I felt dumb for buying into the scenario that strippers and prostitutes were uneducated and sleazy. Well how sweet it was to have the tender moments with Cody's broke ass. I loved him and he loved me, but the bills were still stacked up at my apartment waiting for me. By the time he had a little money I never reaped the rewards from being a loyal "good girl". Not a card, no dinner, no movies, *nothing*. All I got out of the entire situation was a chocolate cake I devoured that I had bought for him on his birthday anyway. So whose really the dumb ass? The women that stick by broke men for love like I was, or the women that prostitute and get a check at the end of the night? At least a prostitute gets paid for her time, and doesn't have to deal with a broken heart. I hated being a woman. I hated the role of being perfect, virtuous, and every version of what others considered lady-like. I had a caramel complexion and I was proud of being Black, but I was starting to resent the trouble that came along with the color of my skin. I got tired of people at work looking at me like I was crazy if I turned the radio to a soft rock station. One white lady actually came up to me and stated she thought all black people listened to Rap music. Some of the white women in the office would actually start rolling their necks as though they were making a mockery of my "blackness", when they asked me the simplest question. I guess they called themselves trying to "act out their version of being black," even though I had no problems with articulation nor did I speak in "Ebonics." Maybe my life would've been easier if I were a White Man. Anna walked by my desk with her layered shoulder-length, thin bleach-blonde damaged hair and her six month pregnant belly. She was mid-thirties, very opinionated with a heart shaped face, pouty lips, and a long parrot-shaped nose. Her makeup was thickly pasted on her face to hide her acne, and her bright red lipstick was an unappealing contrast against her pale skin. She was the sister-in-law of my manager, Ella. So she was given a pass on all of her late absences, doctor's appointments, repeated mistakes, and two hour lunches. She handed me a file so thick, I wanted to throw it back at her. I took the file from her and she forced a smile at me that revealed no teeth.

"Thanks, Erica."

"You're welcome."

"Oh my, Erica I've been meaning to ask you a question."

"I'm listening."

"Why don't black people like to take aspirin?"

"I'm not sure what you mean Anna, because I take aspirin-but I can't answer for every black person." "No silly, because you guys don't want to pick the cotton out of the bottle first!"

This bitch was laughing hysterically and all I could do was stare at her in silence. I guess she noticed the look on my face and knew it was best to shut up immediately. If she wasn't pregnant, I know I would have reached up and slapped the shit out of her. Damn this job, I was so upset my hands were shaking.

"Erica, I was just playing I wasn't trying to upset you, jeez learn to take a joke!" I sat in silence and stared at her so hard she could feel the tension. She decided to remove herself away from my angry glare and scurried away like a timid mouse. I had spent so much time last night reminiscing on my last sexual encounter I realized how long I had gone without sex. After checking my voicemails, I started emailing temps to see if they were available for the upcoming clerical assignments I had to fill for clients. I was trying to find the proper daydream to put my mind at ease, because Anna's remarks had pissed me off. Unfortunately, I knew that going to the "Ella the Elephant" manager to complain about her beloved sister-in-law, Anna, would not work in my favor. I wish there was some way I could put a stick of dynamite in the building and blow it up without being incarcerated. *Yeah, I should think about sex instead.* What a shame women had to be analyzed, ridiculed, accused of mental illness, and every other name in the book on internet blogs if they had sexual desires that did not involve commitment. How long was I suppose to suppress the urge if I didn't want to be married? The double standards were pissing me off even more because I was horny. I never talked anyone into being against marriage so why was I so judged for being single? Could I just find a male friend on the regular that I could also go to the movies with and hang out that would please me sexually as well? No, because I'm Saved and I can't fornicate, only men can without judgment or being labeled as a ho. *Maybe I should break down and finally buy a vibrator.* Dang, a fake dick just seemed completely awkward. What would I do? Would I just say to the salesperson behind the counter, *"Umm, yes, excuse me I would like to purchase 10 inches please."* And what kind of dirty talk would you do to the fake dick? If I'm the one manipulating it then what would I do, call out my own name? *Or would I say, ooohhh yaahhh! That's right, "yah, that's a nice rubber battery dick! give it to me you big fake dick!"* But what if the moisture in my private parts ignited with the battery and caused an electrocution of some sort? I could imagine the hospital calling my mother with that information. *"Yes, excuse me Mrs. Lovelace, are you Erica's mother? This is Doctor Hamilton. I don't know how to tell you this, but it seems as though Erica is being treated for electrocuting her vagina with a vibrator because the battery had a shortage. She is in intensive care right now if you would like to visit."* NOPE. There will be no vibrator action, the hell with that idea.

"Erica...Erica! Yooohooo! I have been standing here for minutes trying to get your attention! What are you thinking about homeslice? Now come on sister girrrlll, you gon give me that file back real quick that I just gave you? I'll give it back in a second, thanks!" Right after she took the file she looked at me with a smirk on her face and rolled her neck. As another employee walked past her, she greeted them in her normal voice, making sure I heard the change in her voice. She was still a few feet away from me and looking at me from the corner of her eye. I was getting sick of Anna's comments. I had to figure out what type of revenge I should seek. Maybe I would volunteer to make her a cup of coffee and spit in it-that would serve the bitch right. I was suppose to meet with William for lunch tomorrow, and maybe he could give me some advice on how to handle the situation at work. I was smart enough to know I could file a complaint on Anna, but I just didn't see the rainbow at the end of the lightening being that Anna and my manager were related. My immediate supervisor on my team had the right idea by leaving this hell-hole. I wonder if she was pretending to like working with me just to keep the peace or if she hated me. She left all of her paperwork so scattered it left me stressed the moment I walked into the office. It was almost time for my shift to end, and I decided that maybe I should go to the bookstore after work. Maybe I would be inspired by some self-help book to see how I could figure out a plan for my life. I wasn't interested in going back to school because I already had a degree in Human Resources, and I hated it. I already knew my problem, I just didn't know how to fix it. There wasn't a lot of money as an actress unless you were a famous one because it was unsteady and unpredictable. Unfortunately, I hadn't found anything else in life that would replace the passion I felt when I stepped on the stage or in front of a camera. I had the common sense to know I couldn't make a living off of it unless I found a magic agent in Hollywood or unless Hollywood came to me. I couldn't keep taking off work to go to auditions, so my agent stopped calling me. I decided to check my personal email before I left for the day. We weren't suppose to log in and use personal email on company time, but I was too excited and wanted to see if the company I had sent my resume to had responded. If I had to stay in Corporate America, at least I would prefer to go somewhere far away from Anna and Ella. When I opened my email, I saw a message from William. I didn't want to start opening too many emails just so Anna or another idiot walking by my desk would catch me in the act. *Well, maybe William wants to let me know what time to meet him so we can discuss the script he wrote.* I scanned through all of my unopened emails. Damn it. I saw no reply from the job I sent my resume to. My heart sank, and I felt like screaming. To say life had so many options, I felt trapped. My mood went so far down I didn't care who walked by anymore. It was almost time for me to get off work anyway. I opened the email from William and I almost fell out of my chair.

"Hi, I am William's sister. I have never met you but he always spoke so highly of you. William went home to be with the Lord late last night. He was a devoted family man, friend, and a wonderful brother. Additional information on his funeral services will be forwarded to you after necessary arrangements have been made."

This had to be a sick joke. I picked up my phone and dialed William's number. I got his voicemail. I called again, no answer. I dialed his number repeatedly until his voicemail was full and I could not leave a message. My heart was beating out of my chest, and I couldn't breathe. I felt dizzy, disoriented, and I was sweating profusely. I immediately grabbed my purse and walked out of the office without even logging off of my computer. I pressed the elevator buttons, holding my chest trying to catch my breath. As soon as got off the elevator I could see it was raining heavily outside. I ran towards my car as fast as I could, wanting to drive to William's house. Tears were falling down my face, rain was hitting my forehead and every inch of my body. The water from the puddles I ran through soaked my shoes and my ankles. I got in my car and started speeding off, and quickly turned on my windshield wipers. I couldn't remember which way to turn,

I still hadn't been able to catch my breath, and I could barely see through the rain on my windows even though my windshield wipers were going as fast as they could. All of the streets I turned on looked foreign to me. The pain in my chest began to be unbearable to the point I had to pull over in front of a park I didn't even recognize. All of a sudden my red mustang was too small for me, and I felt claustrophobic. I parked my car and looked for the nearest tree just to get some fresh air. I dialed William's number again. This time a woman picked up the phone.

"This is Erica, is William there?"

"No, Erica, he's not here anymore. This is William's sister. I left you an email honey, he passed away last night sweetie." She started to cry uncontrollably and hung up the phone. I didn't care who was looking at me, or how many strangers thought I had lost my mind. I tried to take a few more steps but the pain in my chest grew more extreme and I started to vomit. I could see from the corner of my eyes there were silhouettes of strangers walking by looking at me with disgust, as if perhaps I had one too many drinks at a happy hour. I walked a few steps further, and even though it was muddy outside I still didn't care that my new grey and black two piece suit was now sitting in the wet grass full of mud under the tree. Someone had to be playing an awful joke. He had to still be alive. I was suppose to meet him for lunch tomorrow. Why would God take a beautiful person like William away and leave the pedophiles, rapists, and killers on the earth to live such a long life? I felt myself shaking so much I knew that I was having some form of either an anxiety attack or a panic attack. I sat under that tree for hours with my head down over my knees with my arms covering my head until it was so dark outside I could no longer see.

I woke up in the morning to a loud alarm. I had no recollection of driving home, climbing my steps, or laying down. I had on my pajamas but I never remembered pulling off my clothes, it was a complete out of body experience. I had completely blacked out a whole window of time. I knew I was not mentally able to handle going to work today. I could not handle Ella the Elephant or Anna's bitchiness or racial slurs, so I called in to let them know I would be absent that day. I checked my messages and William's sister gave me the address as to where William would be buried. After hearing her voice and having her give the details of his death, I could not get out of bed at that moment. She said he had a blood clot in his leg that no one knew of. Somehow the circulation in his heart was affected by it and he died in his sleep. I cried again and again until my eyelids were in pain and I was developing a migraine. There was no way in hell I was going to that funeral because I refused to look at him leaving me behind. Somewhere in my brain I had to believe that he went away for awhile and that I would see him again. If I looked at him in an open casket or saw his casket lowered into the ground it would be too final. I couldn't pretend I was the stereotype of a strong, black woman. I was weak and I couldn't even lift my head off of my pillow. I reached my arm towards the nightstand and turned on the television. There was a commercial advertising about increasing the intensity of male sexual performance by some magic pill. I never could understand why there was always a remedy to keep a man's dick hard and never a cure for cancer. I heard my phone ringing and debated whether I should even answer it. I picked up the phone since I saw that it was Kelly. I thought she was just calling to check on my and send her condolences. Unfortunately, with the bad news of William's death, I had completely forgot that tonight was Terry's engagement party. I didn't want to go, but I knew that if I didn't get out of bed and get out of the house, I would probably stay in the bed and call in to work all week.

DOUBLE LIVES

I always knew that Terry was a complex individual. She was a hairstylist who managed to keep to herself, single mother of two boys, ages four and nine. Always opinionated, generous, honest and reliable. Despite of not having her children's father around, she always seemed to be financially secure and went to Church every Sunday. She drove a Lincoln Navigator, took vacations twice a year, had lavish parties every year on her birthday and on New Years, and had designer clothes. She was a beautiful Puerto Rican woman of 33 years old and had been dating an Attorney named Derrick for the past two years who she claimed treated her well. She described him to me as an attractive African American male who was 5'10" with a caramel complexion, who was also an Entrepreneur who worked with Real estate on the side. However, I had found it extremely strange that I had never met him over the past two years to say Terry and I had been friends for eight years. Terry wanted to introduce her fiancé that night. Even though her friends had never met him, she did speak of Derrick constantly. She claimed she didn't want to "jinx" the relationship as she had done so many times before. In the past, when she thought her previous situations were more serious than they were, she would introduce her new mate to her friends and family. Months later when the relationship was over, she would get embarrassed and hated to be questioned why her relationship ended. As with most friends that are in a relationship, she insisted that I met Derrick's friend Ricky. He was an Accountant who she claimed was handsome. I wasn't looking for any type of hook up but I tried to have an open mind. I wasn't shallow by any means, but Terry and I didn't share the same taste in men so I was apprehensive. She and I shared the same skeptical nature, so she emailed me a picture of him. Ricky actually looked attractive to my surprise. He wasn't smiling in the picture but he had a handsome face, bald head, beautiful brown skin and a very edgy look. I couldn't see his body from the picture but he appeared to be fit proportionally. She sent him a picture of me as well and reported back to me that he found me to be attractive.

I felt as though I had managed to cover up my pain and puffy eyes from all the crying I had done that day. I arrived at Terry's immaculate five bedroom, 4 bathroom house that was landscaped beautifully. She had a swimming pool, jacuzzi, and a large back yard. I wore a blue, low-cut cocktail dress that showed a reasonable amount of cleavage and landed right above the knee with matching blue stilettos. I went through the trouble of putting spirals in my shoulder-length hair, fuchsia lipstick, and silver earrings. I walked up to Terry and gave her a tight hug and handed her the bottle of Champagne that I had stopped and bought for her. She told me she would be happy to drink half of it tonight since her kids were with their Grandmother so her sons wouldn't have to see her tipsy. She was in a hurry to introduce me to Derrick and I could barely walk fast enough to keep up with her as she rushed to his side. He wore an outfit that closely resembled the clothing that the Brothers wear for the Nation of Islam. He wore a bowtie, brown suit, and a hat. He was an attractive male with very intense eyes, and a nonchalant yet calm demeanor. He quickly shook my hand and smiled but he had the presence of a man that would rather be somewhere else. He sipped on his drink but constantly looked at his watch and was quite fidgety. Something about his spirit rubbed me the wrong way. But as with many women that are in a relationship, they always believe their single friends are "hating" so I debated on whether to say anything at all. Besides, I knew that Terry thought Derrick was God's gift to women. Even though she never brought him around, I had the feeling that he could do no wrong in her eyes. She bragged too much on how involved he was with Church. He went every Sunday, they prayed together, and he made her dinner twice a week. On several occasions when she went to Church with him, she told me that she witnessed him catching the "Holy Ghost". Not to mention, I was pretty confused on why I could detect something wrong with someone else's man. How come my radar didn't ever flash quickly enough when it ME dating a man I was in a relationship with? I noticed from the corner of my eye that the man walking up to Terry, Derrick, and I looked a lot like the picture I saw of Ricky. They say a picture is worth a thousand words but the one Terry showed me wasn't worth enough words. He walked up to me, took my hand and gently kissed it. Then he embraced Terry with a big hug and gave Derrick a firm handshake. Ricky turned his attention to me and said, "What it do Shawty?" I laughed and said, "I'm fine." I have no idea why so many Black men use Ebonics as a greeting. He started asking me the usual screening questions that never cease to annoy me. "Do you have a man, do you have any children, do you have a job?" I felt like I was in a job interview but I guess the screening process is a necessary evil. He finally smiled and I couldn't help but notice he had extremely buck teeth. I could see the top row but I could not locate the bottom row. I didn't mean to focus my attention on it but the more he talked the more I searched. I had plenty of time to search because he kept bragging about his car, his house, his money, his boat, his timeshares, and his new business he was opening. I kept laughing at all his jokes just so I could keep him laughing to do my own personal examination. I finally saw the bottom row of teeth, and miraculously the entire bottom row of his teeth was in a gangster lean in a 45 degree angle. I wouldn't consider the lack of perfection as a deal breaker because no one is perfect. I'm not a woman that thinks I'm "all of that". What turned me off is that he continued to brag on so much of his material possessions I couldn't figure out why he wouldn't make the investment on his teeth. After becoming mesmerized at his mouth, I snapped out of my hypnotized state when he made the comment that I was "cute", but he preferred white women or women that were of lighter complexion. I guess my caramel complexion was not light enough. I excused myself from the ignorant bastard and decided to look around if Kelly had arrived. I heard Ricky

yelling behind me, "hey, I like dark girls too!"
It's a shame with all the money he bragged on,
he forgot to purchase some class. Terry was
mingling with the crowd and had made eye
contact with me to search my expression for
feedback on Ricky. I rolled my eyes at her and
she gave me a shrug from across the room. I
decided to go to the kitchen and sit on one of
her barstools to have a drink alone. My mind
was drifting because I was bored and I couldn't
get my mind off William. After two margaritas
I walked out of the kitchen and headed towards
the bathroom. On my way there, Terry stopped
me and asked if I had seen Derrick. I told her I
hadn't seen him and I would let him know she
was looking for him if I bumped into him. I
hoped that by walking around I wouldn't run
into Ricky. Terry had an extremely large living
room and game room downstairs. There were
about fifty guests in her home and they were
scattered everywhere like roaches. I made my

way to the restroom and someone was in there because it was locked. I decided to go upstairs to one of her other restrooms instead of waiting around downstairs to take a piss. As I walked upstairs and passed by her bedroom, I could clearly hear noises that sounded like a dog grunting. Terry was downstairs, so who would be in her bedroom? I had known Terry for years, and even I never invaded her privacy by going in her bedroom when she wasn't present. Something told me to open the door, but I kept walking towards the bathroom. The noises were getting louder, and it was coming from two different people. What if they were trying to lift her big screen TV or rob her and I chose to go to the bathroom and not say or do anything? What kind of friend would I be? I tiptoed towards the bedroom and slightly opened the door. I turned on the light and screamed at the top of my lungs. *OHHHHH SHIT!!* Derrick was standing up with his pants down to his ankles and his shirt off, while Ricky was on his knees butt-naked sucking Derrick's dick. I had startled both of them with my scream and they immediately started scrambling to put their clothes back on. I ran down the steps and headed towards the door. I couldn't say bye to Terry. How would I explain that her fiancé was getting his dick sucked by the fool she tried to hook me up with right in her bedroom? I couldn't take the time to rummage through the guests to find Kelly, I had to get the hell out of there-immediately. How sick could Derrick be to do that right upstairs in Terry's bedroom while his engagement party was taking place? Was he THAT drunk? Unfortunately, Terry ran after me on the way to my car asking me what was wrong. She had such a confused look on her face standing there with the champagne bottle I bought for her engagement party. "Erica, I was just about to open this champagne, where are you going all upset like that? Did that fool Ricky piss you off chica?" I hated to be the one to break the news to her. She looked so happy and so many people were in her house I just didn't know what do. Was I suppose to let her believe that her fiancé was heterosexual and marry him knowing what I knew? If I prolonged telling her, how pissed would she be if she slept with him tonight and I knew about his homosexual activities in her bedroom and chose not to disclose that to her? Terry always knew when I wasn't telling the truth, so sooner or later I would have to say something. This was a no-win situation. When I broke the news to her she stood there in silence. I expected her to be in tears, but she just looked me in the eyes and stared at me for what seemed an eternity, and mumbled "thank you for telling me." I had wondered if she even believed me when I told her what I saw. Her face looked evil, disgusted, and solemn. As she turned her back and walked towards her home, I wondered if I should follow after her. I called out to her to ask her if she would be okay. No answer. Her demeanor made me nervous as hell because she had the look of a woman that was capable of blowing up her own house. I stood outside my car and decided to wait from a distance where I can see her. Derrick met her at the door and stood outside with a sheepish grin as if nothing was wrong. She whispered something in his ear and he immediately looked towards me and screamed, *"YOU BITCH, ERICA YOU'RE A FUCKING LYING BITCH!"* Terry stood there beside him in silence, with a blank look on her face as she stared at me. I immediately cursed myself internally for saying anything at all. Evidently, somewhere in her mind she believed I would make up a story like that on her groom to be. Just as Derrick and Terry left to walk back into the house, Ricky met them at the door with tears in his eyes. "Derrick, don't you think we've lied to ourselves long enough? Why don't you tell your woman about us? I'm tired of playing this game-lying, sneaking around, and being your shameful secret! Fuck this! Enough! Are you in love with me or this bitch?" Terry took the champagne bottle and immediately clocked it over Derrick's head and kicked him straight in his balls. I don't know if it was Derrick or Ricky who screamed the loudest over the initial shock of Terry's attack.

JUDGEMENT DAY

I wanted to get Terry out of jail but I couldn't. The incident at Terry's house was so loud, the neighbors had called the police and she was arrested. On the one phone call she made, she let me know that I did the right thing by telling her because she needed to know before she made the mistake of marrying a man on the down low. She told me where her children were and made sure they were with their Grandmother, and told me to tell them she loved them. I thought Terry would just be held on assault charges, but little did I know she had warrants for identity theft. Terry never had custody of her two sons, so she stole someone's identity to hide from her ex-husband in Puerto Rico. Her real name was Jennifer Robles, but for eight years I knew her as Terry Sanchez. She had managed to fool everyone the eight years we had been friends, but to me-she was still Terry. She was the loving, supporting, friend I came to know and I had no judgment in my heart towards her. I often wondered how she could afford the type of house she had but I'm not the type of person to question people about their personal finances. I didn't know what type of high paying clients she had at the salon and I thought maybe she was getting some form of child support that helped her financially. But there are going to be things you don't know about a person no matter how long you know them. I didn't understand how she accumulated a beautiful home, car, vacations, and designer clothing being a single mother of two children on someone else's identity; but we can't always see what goes on beneath the flesh of another human being-even though the cliché exists that the eyes are the window to the soul. I thought I had enough tears shed over William, and I was emotionally drained as it was-now I had another situation to depress me.

When I talked to Kelly, she said she had left me several messages telling me she couldn't take off work to be at the Engagement party, but I probably couldn't hear my cell phone over the music and loud guests. Kelly broke out in loud sobs over the phone when I told her the news. We both tried to come up with a plan to split the cost to bail out Terry before her trial even though both of us were low on funds. I woke up that morning looking at the pile of clothes in my laundry basket with hatred, wishing they could magically wash themselves. I reached over to grab my phone and called into work once again. All I wanted to do was stay in bed, go to sleep, and wake up again so that the last few days would be just a bad dream so everything would turn back to normal. But then again, nothing about me would be considered normal before that anyway. I got up to load my washing machine and noticed there was no detergent. *Shit,* I was hungry and my refrigerator was empty as well. The last thing I wanted to do was go to the grocery store but I had no choice.

When I walked down the aisles of the grocery store, I completely understood why people say never to shop while you're hungry. My basket was piled with all sorts of chips, cookies, ice cream; things I know I shouldn't indulge in-but I was not in the mood to care. After the clerk took my cash and gave me back my change, I felt stupid when I looked at all the grocery bags that I knew I couldn't carry with two hands. The bagger had taken my cart as if I no longer needed it so he could give it to another shopper. I was walking a little slower to keep my bags in place to prevent from dropping anything right when a Caucasian lady bumped into me. She had shoulder-length brown uncombed hair, about 5' 7", chubby, with a green tank top too small for her frame, orange shorts that exposed her cellulite, and cheap purple sunglasses. She was on her cell phone carrying all of two bags, completely nonchalant and oblivious to bumping into me. Much to my irritation, there was no apology as one of my bags fell to the floor spilling out four navel oranges. I scrambled to pick them up and put them back into my grocery bag. A black gentleman appearing to be in his late twenties-early thirties stepped right over my hand while I was picking up the oranges and ran behind the Caucasian brunette to offer the "damsel in distress" his loving black hand to assist her in carrying her *two* bags. As I put the last orange back into my bag, I rearranged the laundry detergent under my armpit and put five of my bags in each hand. As I walked back to my mustang, right across from my car the black "gentleman" was standing at the Caucasian brunette's Chevy Pickup putting her two bags in the passenger side. I didn't understand how he felt she needed more help than I with her arms so free of weight, compared to the load I was carrying. History definitely repeats itself. Slavery taught so many black men to serve the white women and overlook the black women they were chained to. Black women were expected to be so strong, that sometimes we suppress the vulnerabilities and emotions every woman has because we are not given the permission by society to express ourselves without being put into a stereotype. Finally, when we break free we are classified as too independent, aggressive, or we are told we have attitudes. Why didn't I ever need any help? Was I "too strong" to need assistance? All those stupid blogs on the internet with people say Black women have attitudes. How was I giving him any attitude by picking up my oranges off of the floor? It's not a big deal that the black gentleman might have chosen to help the Caucasian Brunette with her grocery bags first.

It was a big deal because he did nothing but look at me, walk off, and never offered any assistance before walking his black ass into those sliding doors. The incident reminded me all too well of all the Black men I had come across that said black women were too independent. Yet, if we became dependent on them, we would be left to carry the load-just like these damn grocery bags I had to carry anyways. *I'm glad I am strong enough to carry my own bags, brother.* I got in my car after loading my grocery bags in the trunk and drove off. All of the negative books and articles I read about black women started to float in my head while I drove home. *"Black women are too picky, they need to keep their mouths closed, you're too light-skinned, you're too dark-skinned, your hair is too nappy, "settle" over "single", be "submissive", "change your attitude", you argue too much, you're too loud, don't put that weave in your hair even though other races can, don't relax your hair*-be what we say you are even if you're not, and do what we tell you to be just so you can snatch up some self-entitled son of a bitch that was considered to be a "good man" measured by his own self worth. All a man had to have was a car and a job. His requirements were so futile. For some reason I couldn't buy into the vicious propaganda that so many women and men of African American decent were buying into. I never saw any articles or books where a White man bashed ALL white women, but I did see countless brothers and sisters debating relationship requirements and putting each other down. When I got to my apartment, I unloaded my car and took my grocery bags upstairs. At that moment I wished that I was White. Not for a lifetime to disinherit my race, but just for a moment. I wanted to feel privileged. I was tired of being grouped, stereotyped, judged, and persecuted for every word that came out of my mouth and every decision I made. I didn't want to hear that I was disinheriting my race just because I wore a relaxer. Every single race gets to wear their hair the way they damn well please, yet I had ran into too many neo-soul sisters that were preaching how I should give up my relaxer, as if the black would erase off my skin if my hair was straight. It's funny how so many Black people claim they want rights and freedom yet those very same Black people try to put restrictions on each other's identity. It's sad that I couldn't be a little White princess free from all the drama, just for a moment. I could scream, be loud, be whatever I wanted to be and someone would still look at me as an individual. They would take my childhood, relationships, career, and everything into consideration before they passed judgment on me. I couldn't figure out why Vanessa Williams had to give up her Miss USA pageant crown for some photos she took in her past, yet Donald Trump gave the Blonde-haired, blue eyed innocent Caucasian woman another chance to keep her Miss USA crown after she was using drugs. The rules and freedom were stripped for me and my caramel complexion, sociology and media had turned people into puppets. I was not allowed to choose whether or not I wanted children without the stares of those tied down into motherhood looking at me as though I was selfish, yet they complained daily about their issues and lack of freedom. I would be persecuted by married individuals even though they were in a loveless marriage just because I chose to remain single. No matter what I read or what other people say, my mind could not wrap around the purpose of me getting married again. Just because a man had a house, car, and a job I should be submissive and wait on him hand and foot? Why? I had a place to live, car, and a job my damn self. It wasn't out of arrogance, conceit, or because I was a "black woman" or being too "independent", I just didn't see the *reason*. The more I didn't see it, the more people would throw Bible verses at me as if I were the walking Antichrist. Yet they had no problems having children out of wedlock, drinking, and acting a damn fool when they pleased while passing judgment on others. I guess God excused them from all of their daily mistakes or choices in life. I would be nominated in an all-White corporate environment at my job to speak for and represent all black people as they watched every tiny move I made so that judgment could pass from their lips the moment I made a mistake. I looked at the time and realized that Kelly was suppose to stop by in a few minutes. I would have been happy to see her, but I had no energy for company. I picked up the phone to cancel and started to dial her number just as I heard a knock on the door. *Damn, she was at the door already.* As I put down the phone and walked to the door I felt weak. I had been too drained to keep crying and I knew Kelly was very emotional. I had no energy to be strong for her. As soon as I opened the door, a fist came at me dead in my nose. It hurt so bad I immediately fell to the floor. I tried to scream but for some reason it felt as though I couldn't scream loud enough. I tried to lift my head up for a split second to see the face and immediately saw it was Derrick. I was too weak to stand so I crawled away from him. He came up behind me and grabbed me by the hair while he stood over me. He kicked me in my back, stomach, ribs, and chest for what seemed like an eternity. I was balled up in a fetal position with one arm over my face and I could barely breathe. His kicks were knocking the wind out of me. I was already weak before I opened the door, and as beaten down as I felt, I knew I had to fight even though I had no strength. For the split second he stopped kicking me, all I could hear was him calling me every name in the book as my lifeless stiff body lie still while he held a tight grip on my hair. *"Bitch! Stupid ass ho! You think you was gonna get away with breaking up my fucking engagement! You just couldn't mind your own fucking business!"* His words and his fists represented *Life* itself, and I was tired of *Life* beating me down. In that split second, I took the arm that had been covering my face and punched him with all my strength directly in his balls. I felt him lose a grip on my hair as he doubled over holding his nuts. With the last fleeting moment of energy I had, I stood up and quickly grabbed a stool by the kitchen and knocked him over the head with it. As he instantly fell to the floor, I could hear him screaming like a bitch trying to hide his face the same way I had tried to cover mine just seconds before. I hit him with the stool several times before I put it down. I wasn't going to stop until I saw him bleed. I picked up the vase on my table and leaned over him and started beating him upside his head repeatedly until my arms grew even weaker as they were before. It still wasn't enough revenge for me. This silly motherfucker had caught me on the wrong day. Here I was trying to get over the loss of William and Terry's double life that landed her in prison. Yet Derrick had the nerve to come to *my* house unannounced trying to beat me to a pulp after playing the role of a Holy Church member? After playing my friend Terry, knowing he was a down-low brother, and he's calling me every name in the book? I took a lamp off my table and smashed it over his head. As soon as I saw he wasn't moving I rushed to the kitchen to get a knife and ran to my phone to dial 911. Derrick seemed to be unconscious but I yelled at him from a few feet away that if he moved one inch I would stab him.

The police and the ambulance came to my apartment about seven minutes later. Derrick was now conscious even though his face was bloody from the blows to his head. He was still cursing at me under his breath as the paramedic checked his injuries and the police took him out in handcuffs. The paramedics checked me as well to see if I had any serious injuries. They recommended I go to the hospital to get a more in-depth checkup to make sure I had no internal injuries from all of the kicks I suffered to my abdomen. I filled out a police report and let the officer know I wanted to press charges. He told me I would need to go to the police station as soon as possible to fill out more paperwork. I shut the door behind them and went straight to the bathroom mirror to look at what possible damage was done to my face. My nose was still bleeding but it wasn't broken. I didn't have any extreme injuries on my face. I didn't know if it was because I covered my head while I was attacked, or because Derrick had spent so much time kicking me in my stomach.

At least the severity of the attack was not showing on my face.

I decided to go to work the next day. I had called in one time too many. I still needed time off, but I knew the work was piling up. I had went down to the police station to fill out all of the necessary paperwork to press charges that night. It did give me a wicked sense of pleasure to know that my few scars could be covered with makeup, yet when Derrick left in handcuffs his face looked like he was the one who received the home invasion. He was way more bruised than me-thanks to the kitchen stool, lamp, and heavy vase. I walked into work the next day without speaking to anyone, I just went straight to my desk and turned on the computer. The files on my desk were stacked up higher than a full deck of cards. Ella came up to my desk crunching on her chips shoveling them into her mouth and just looked at me. "The next time you need a vacation you need to let me know in advance so I can approve it. We can't run this office on "CP" time. I don't care how much *you people* push for affirmative action, you've got to work like everyone else." I could feel my adrenaline rising as I looked at her. There was no expression on her clueless pumpkin face. No one gave a damn that I had been doing the job of two people after my other supervisor had left. No one cared all of the hours I stayed later than I had to. No one cared that I hadn't even taken a vacation or had any sick days the whole year up until this past week. Everyone else got to call in when their children were sick, meanwhile I had to pick up the slack when they were out for weeks on end. I'm the one who did two jobs when a fellow female co-worker decided to go on maternity leave. I always put my head down, did the work, shut my mouth, and played their little office politics games. I dealt with their sly racist remarks and their belittling comments long enough and I wanted to get off of the plantation. In a calm voice I said, "Look you fat fuckbasket, I am tired of your racist ass office and your superior attitude."

"Look here Erica, you need to watch your mouth!" she replied.

"No *bitch*, why don't you watch your *weight*? Better yet, watch *this!*"

I threw all of the files piled on my desk onto the floor. Hundreds of pieces of paper landed everywhere while she looked at me in shock. I grabbed my purse and walked towards the door and left Ella standing there to pick up the pieces of paper off the floor. I got into the elevator before I started crying. I had no box to pack before leaving because I wasn't like the thousands of people in Corporate America that put up pictures and personal belongings in their cubicle, knowing we are in an economy that has chronic unexpected layoffs. When I got in my car and drove home I felt scared, yet free. As soon as I opened the door to my apartment, I made myself a cup of Chai tea. So many thoughts were running through my head at once. I wanted to pick up the phone and cry out to my mom and dad like a helpless child in need, but the last thing I wanted to do is worry them. I also knew they would tell me I was a fool for quitting my job in this bad economy. They would tell me what types of discrimination they faced, that were far worse than mine when they were younger. I would be told that I was living in a fantasy and that my expectations were too unrealistic. They would tell me that Terry shouldn't have taken her sons when she didn't have custody, so what she did that got her arrested was her fault. They would ignore the fact that it still left me in pain because I lost a friend. They would tell me to be strong and move on. My anger and pain would stay bottled inside me because I had no way to release it. After all, I couldn't use my creativity as an outlet. I had to get a job and be responsible. I pulled off my clothes after finishing my cup of tea and got in the shower. As I stood there in the water, I was so disoriented I didn't know if my face was wet from tears or from the warm water dripping down on me. I had turned 30 and I was nowhere near what I thought I would be at this point in my life. When I thought of my high-school graduation day and the list of accomplishments I wrote down, there were many left undone. But through all the pain, I had survived it, with God on my side. I got out of the shower and looked in the mirror through the foggy precipitation from the hot shower.

I made smears on the mirror with my hand so I could see my reflection. I wasn't a perfect supermodel, but God blessed me with an attractive face. I was a cinnamon brown skinned black woman, proportioned, and a free-spirited intelligent non-conformist. I would never able to enjoy the privileges that only came to famous Blacks and Caucasian people. But I could not allow the world to tell me what I am suppose to be as a woman or as a Black human being when they have never met me as an individual. I am what I am. My hair is coarse and thick, I have full lips. God blessed me with a mother who loved me unconditionally and a Father who was responsible enough to provide for his children. No, I don't belong in an office, but I probably have to go back to Corporate America real soon so I can pay my bills. My heart was so heavy, I did something I hadn't done in a while. There I was, butt-naked with my face on the floor, I got down on my knees and cried. Not about all the bad things that had happened the past few days, but for all the things I was blessed with that God gave me. He gave me talent and my own unique personality, even if society would continue to put me in a box based on my black skin. They didn't know me beneath my flesh. They didn't know my thoughts, they couldn't have my soul, and I begged for Jesus to forgive me for all the times I silently regretted having my caramel brown skin. I wasn't at Church every Sunday to prove anything to anyone, but I had my own personal time with Jesus. I asked the Lord for comfort to deal with the passing of William, who I felt was the only man that truly understood me. I felt a peace and a joy come over me just like the day I felt when I got Saved and joined Church years ago. After getting off my knees and wiping my tears, I put on some clothes. At that moment I recalled William's words telling me *"if I haven't given up then why should you?"* William didn't get the chance to finish some of the scripts he told me about. He didn't get to finish the soundtrack for the Independent film he was going to produce. His dreams and his talents were buried with him and I needed to live at least some of my dreams while I was still alive. If I could just find the strength to follow my heart while I was still breathing, my eccentricity would not be in vain. I went to my computer to check my email. I didn't get a reply in my inbox for the job I applied to, but I received an audition notice passed along to me from a former actor I had done a production with years ago. I wasn't sure if I was ready for anymore disappointment if I didn't get the role, but I was going anyway. I was going to follow my dreams, and if anyone had a problem with it they could kiss my Black ass. After all, I'm free.

"Beneath My Flesh"

Acknowledgement Page:

Thank you to my parents who gave me their best,
Thank you for my siblings who I ran to when I felt
judged or distressed.
Thank you for my friends that have walked with
me through my troubles,
Thank you to all of those who God removed from
my life because you weren't equipped to walk with
me through my struggles.
Thank you for my friend Warren, who is sleeping
peacefully in heaven,
Thank you for my Godfather who is singing his
favorite song, "Standing on the Dock in the bay"
hope I make it into Heaven so I can see you one
day.
Rest in Peace Godfather.
Thank you for my nieces and nephews that may be
far away yet so close to my heart.
To my Grandparents, I didn't have enough time to
get to know you before the Lord took you to rest
but just know your Grand-daughter thinks of the
moments I spent with you when I was just a young
little pest.
Thanks to the Aunties and Uncles that made a
place for me when I came to visit. The distance has
not been a great friend to us, but even though we
barely get to meet-
You made me feel at home, like we never parted;
its as if all those years I was living right across the
street.
Thank you Jesus, for giving me the courage to be
ME.
GINA-NACOLE

ABOUT THE AUTHOR

Gina-Nacole was born in Frankfurt, Germany. She currently resides in Dallas, Texas. In her career, she has worked professionally as a producer and playwright with stage plays such as "A Woman's Intuition", "Love Doctor", and "Sex Changes." She has also worked professionally as a choreographer and actress. She enjoys writing poetry, writing one-act plays, spending time with friends and family, traveling, and playing her flute. BENEATH MY FLESH is her first novel.

"Beneath My Flesh"

<u>**Author's Autograph Page**</u>:

GINA-NACOLE
142

www.ingramcontent.com/pod-product-compliance
Lightning Source LLC
Chambersburg PA
CBHW070557180626
46817CB00005B/1888